EAST RENFREWSHIRE

09

D1512764

ReadZone Books Limited

www.ReadZoneBooks.com

© in this edition 2016 ReadZone Books Limited

This print edition published in cooperation with Fiction Express, who first published this title in weekly instalments as an interactive e-book.

FICTION EXPRESS

Fiction Express
First Floor Office, 2 College Street,
Ludlow, Shropshire SY8 1AN
www.fictionexpress.co.uk

Find out more about Fiction Express on pages 101–102.

Design: Laura Harrison & Keith Williams
Cover Image: Bigstock

© in the text 2015 Andrew G Taylor
The moral right of the author has been asserted.

ISBN 978-1-78322-598-9

Printed in Malta by Melita Press

BEING SUPER

ANDREW G TAYLOR

What do other readers think?

Here are some comments left on the Fiction Express blog about this book:

[I've] just finished Being Super. *I liked all the action."*
Anna, Kirkwall

From readers at Moray School Falkirk:

"We love your book Being Super *because it always has a new challenge and it is definitely a page turner."*
Izzy

"Being Super was great. It was full of action with explosions and gadgets. In the future, I would like a movie."
Mia

"I really liked Being Super *because it always left me wanting more. Is there going to be a sequel?"*
Christopher

Contents

Chapter 1   Night of the Guardian   7

Chapter 2   "They have dogs"   17

Chapter 3   Shadow Warrior   27

Chapter 4   Trapped!   37

Chapter 5   Tried and Tested   46

Chapter 6   "He's Finished"   56

Chapter 7   Breakout!   63

Chapter 8   Big George   75

Chapter 9   Showdown   81

Chapter 10   "Time to leave"   90

About Fiction Express   101

About the Author   104

Chapter 1

Night of the Guardian

The thieves crouched by the side of the Toyota, keeping out of sight of the nearest house. The younger of the two worked a misshapen coat hanger down the driver's window.

"Get on with it," whispered Kyle as he looked up and down the street.

"I'm going as fast as I can," Dylan, his partner, replied irritably as he wiggled the bent wire down the inside of the door.

"Just smash the window!"

"Look, I saw this on TV. It works!" A second later there was a click as the door lock released. Dylan reached for the door handle…

"STOP!"

The thieves froze in shock as they were bathed in brilliant light. Kyle held up his hand and squinted, making out the silhouette of a figure standing about five metres away.

Dylan dropped the coat hanger. "It's him!"

"Who?" Kyle looked confused.

"The *Guardian Angel*," Dylan hissed.

Kyle gave a snorting laugh. Everyone living in Estruca had heard rumours of the Guardian Angel – some guy walking the streets at night in a suit, fighting crime. Had to be nonsense.

"STEP AWAY FROM THE CAR," the voice of the Guardian Angel boomed from the light. The shadow started walking forwards slowly.

"I'm out of here," yelped Dylan as he bolted into the darkness.

The Guardian Angel watched Dylan flee, then turned back to Kyle.

"RUN!" he commanded.

Kyle's eyes were becoming accustomed to the glare of the light. He could also see that the stranger was muscular… but that could just be padding in the costume. He reached into his pocket, pulling out the hammer he carried for smashing car windows.

"Make me," he growled, flexing his fingers around the handle of the tool. Taking down a local hero would do his street reputation no end of good.

The Guardian Angel's domed head cocked slightly to one side, as if considering the situation. Then, as Kyle tensed to leap forward, his adversary touched something on his wrist….

A screeching, high-pitched whine split the air. Kyle's hands went to cover his ears, but it felt as if the noise was drilling into his brain. He collided with the Toyota.

"HEADACHE?" asked the Angel, his rasping voice adding to the pain coursing through Kyle's skull. "A 17.5 KILOHERTZ BLAST AT THIS RANGE WILL DO THAT."

Kyle wanted to throw himself at his attacker, seeing the shadow advancing on him once more… but the light and the noise was just too much.

With a violent curse, Kyle turned and fled into the night.

* * *

Through his visor, Gabe Gibson watched the second thief run away. The Mosquito had done the trick and the ear protectors in his helmet had shielded him from the worst of the sound. Now Gabe tapped the control screen built into the left arm of his suit to cancel the screech. After a moment, silence returned as neighbourhood pets stopped yowling.

Gabe killed the high-powered lamps built into the suit shoulders with another tap of the control hub. Reaching to his belt as he approached the car, he removed a printed card and slipped it under one of the windscreen wipers. Then, aware that lights were coming on in the nearest house, he turned and ran towards the darkness of the park opposite.

A girl was crouching beside a gum tree at the edge of the park and she held up a phone, filming his approach. Gabe recognized her instantly. Cathy Chen. She was in the same year as him at school, ran the student info blog and considered herself an ace reporter. Gabe wondered how long she'd been following him.

"Turn that off," he ordered. He'd already remodulated the speaker output on his helmet so his voice no longer boomed. However, it still transformed his normal voice, making it deeper and hoarser – like Christian Bale in the *Batman* movies.

Disappointed, Cathy lowered the phone and stood up. "That was amazing! Those guys totally wimped out!" She looked in the direction the thieves had run. "So, you're not going to chase after them?"

"No need." With a tap of the control screen, Gabe brought up the images that his suit camera had captured of the thieves at work on the Toyota. He hit the upload symbol, sending them as an anonymous email to the state police of Victoria.

"What was that sound thing you used on them?"

"I call it the Mosquito," Gabe replied reluctantly, pointing to a device on his belt. "Emits a high-pitched scream that only teenagers and household pets can hear."

Cathy had a notepad and pen in her hand now and was scribbling down details. "Mosquito… Very effective!" She looked up at him. "Tell me more about your..." she waved a hand at him, "super-suit."

Gabe sighed. In normal life, Cathy would never even speak to him. She was part of the in-crowd at Estruca High. Didn't even know he existed… sitting at the back of the class, with Clark, Peter and Bruce, his fellow geeks. But tonight Gabe was the *Guardian Angel*. And Cathy clearly wanted his story.

"I don't think so," he replied curtly. "I'd like you to delete that clip you took on your phone. You didn't have my permission to record it."

Cathy stuck out her chin. "This is a public place. I can film what I like." They faced one another for a moment, on the verge of a serious argument, but then the girl's face softened. "Look, all I want is something for my blog. This story is going to be great publicity! And with the clip of you taking on those car thieves… everyone's gonna go nuts!"

"I don't need any publicity!" growled Gabe, aware of Cathy trying to see through his tinted visor. She was obviously desperate to know his real identity. Gabe was tall for his age and with the foam padding beneath the rubber of his suit, he was pretty sure he passed for someone much older.

"*Everyone* needs publicity!" she continued enthusiastically. "At the moment you're just a rumour. People think the Guardian Angel is just some crazy guy running around after dark in a wetsuit."

Gabe reddened. The super-suit was indeed made from an old wetsuit of his dad's that he'd found abandoned in a closet.

"And the cops want to shut you down as well."

"Really?" said Gabe, suddenly interested. "And how do you know that?"

Cathy bit her lip. "My… uh… dad is a commander in the state police. I overheard him calling the Guardian Angel a vigilante. He says if they catch you, you'll be the one who gets put in jail."

"Great," said Gabe bitterly. If the cops did a better job, he wouldn't need to be out on a school night making sure that the neighbourhood was safe. Everyone knew Estruca was in the grip of a crimewave. His mum's car had been broken into twice in the past few months.

"Come on," Cathy said persuasively. "Just a few more questions and I'll leave you alone. *Promise.* What did you put on the car window?"

Seeing that it was probably the only way to get rid of her, Gabe held out one of the cards from his belt. She took it and examined the printed message:

ANOTHER CRIME PREVENTED BY…
THE GUARDIAN ANGEL

"Nice touch," said Cathy. "Mind if I keep this?" She slipped the card into the notebook before he could respond. She was looking his suit up and down again inquisitively. "Tell me about those lights."

The high-powered cycle lamps built into the shoulders of Gabe's suit were as powerful as car headlights on full beam. He'd bought them online and built them into the suit in his workshop. But Cathy already knew more than enough about his suit he decided, folding his arms across his chest.

At that moment, the command hub on his wrist flashed. He tapped the screen, opening a new message. It was from whistleblower365, the anonymous source who had tipped him off about the car thieves earlier that evening. It read:

Check out the old steelworks. Something more serious than car theft going down. You up for that?

Gabe swiped the message closed and turned back to Cathy. "I have to go."

"I'll come with you."

He shook his head. "I'll be moving too fast."

She looked at him sceptically. "In that outfit?"

"You'd be surprised."

He started off, but she ran after him. Gabe wheeled around, holding out a hand.

"No," he said firmly. "You will not follow."

She gave him a withering look. "How are you going to stop me?"

Gabe gritted his teeth, seeing that she wasn't about to take no for an answer. "Fine… if you can keep up."

"Lead the way."

Chapter 2

"They have dogs"

The Bolton Steelworks had once been *the* employer in Estruca, but it had closed down ten years ago. That's when it had all started going wrong for the town. Unemployment. Poverty. Crime. Now the empty, decaying factory buildings on the edge of town were just a reminder of a richer past.

A four-metre-high security fence ran the perimeter of the factory. The signs warned of dog patrols, but everyone knew the place was unguarded as even the security men had been laid off. Gabe approached it at a run, leaped and scaled the fence smoothly. At the top he swung his body over and jumped down, his landing cushioned by the heavy-duty boots of his suit.

He watched as Cathy came racing up on the other side. She'd matched him stride for stride on the run across town, sticking to the shadows where he had, moving with stealth. He'd secretly been impressed… but now he was interested to see how she handled the fence.

Cathy didn't slow, scrambling up the chain links as quickly as he had. She swung over and landed in a crouch beside him.

She smiled sweetly. "Didn't think I'd keep up, did you?"

Gabe shrugged. "I've been training for this kind of thing. You haven't."

"I'm captain of the school gym team," she replied. "I bet I could outrun and outmanoeuvre you any day."

Gabe rolled his eyes. Cathy was always full of herself at school, too. He wanted to ditch her, but she seemed more than capable of keeping pace with him for the moment. Something told

him it would be better to keep her close –
at least that way he could keep an eye on her.

He looked towards the desolate factory
buildings, stark in the moonlight. They were
red brick, dating back almost a hundred years.
A chill wind whistled over the broken chimney
stacks that towered behind them. Smashed
windows glared like empty eye sockets.

And a light was shining in the centre of
the complex.

"Looks like *someone* is home," said Gabe.

"What are we waiting for?"

They moved off, Gabe leading the way, fast and
low along the perimeter of the complex. As they
came level with the buildings, Gabe made a sprint
across the open ground and pressed himself into
the shadows, breathing hard. Cathy arrived a
second later. She started to move along the wall,
but Gabe caught her arm and shook his head.

"Not through the front door," he whispered,
his voice coming out as a rasp through the
helmet synth.

She looked at him questioningly and he pointed upwards, before moving to a downpipe and starting to climb. The building was three storeys high, but the gloves and the tread of his boots helped. At the top he tested the gutter for strength and then pulled himself on to the sloping, roof. Cathy was right behind him, and they moved across the slate tiles in the direction of a skylight. Crouching at the edge, Gabe looked down through the shattered glass.

The room below was large and dimly lit. He guessed it must have been a storeroom in the past, because there were rusting metal shelves lining the walls. Now it was empty save for a lamp standing in the middle of the floor, illuminating dusty floorboards, and a chair.

Tied to the chair, his head slumped on his chest, was a kid his age.

Cathy stared at the figure, then gasped, "I know him!"

Gabe couldn't admit it without risking giving away that he went to Estruca High, but he recognized the kid too. Iain Thompson. A real jock type, captain of the AFL and the cricket teams. Son of Big George Thompson, the richest guy in Estruca. After the steelworks closed, Big George had moved in and started buying up land. He was just about the most disliked guy in town.... But his son was one of the most popular kids in school.

"His name's Iain Thompson," Cathy confirmed. "He's... he's a friend of mine. Poor Iain!"

Gabe shook his head. Typical that she'd be best friends with a lunkhead like Thompson. Rich kids stuck together and formed the cool crowd, he thought bitterly.

"Yeah, poor Iain," he said.

Something in his tone must have come through the vocal synth, because Cathy looked at him sharply. "Iain's Big George's son, right? Well, he hasn't been in school for over a week. He must have been kidnapped!"

Gabe reached round to the storage compartment on the back of his suit, retrieving the folding grapple he'd made using some old tent pegs. He pressed the button on the side and the hooks sprung out. Attaching this to the edge of the skylight, he let the rope fall down into the room.

"Where did you get a grappling hook?" asked Cathy.

"That's for me to know." Gabe positioned himself in the open skylight and tested the rope. "Wait here and stay out of sight."

Before she could argue, he lowered himself down, sliding the rope between his gloves, using his legs to control his descent. When the rope ran out, Gabe dropped the rest of the way, landing on his tiptoes. Floorboards groaned underfoot and dust rose in the LED light of the lantern.

In the chair, Iain Thompson gave a low moan. As Gabe approached, the boy raised his head, revealing cracked lips and a bruise on his left cheek. His eyes widened as he took in the Guardian Angel.

"I'm here to rescue you," said Gabe.

Iain looked him up and down derisively. "In fancy dress? Is that a motorcycle helmet?"

Gabe was seized by the urge to tip Iain's chair backwards to see if it made him any more polite, when a low growl came from the shadows. Iain's face turned white.

"They have dogs," he said.

Gabe turned to see the blur of an Alsatian leaping. The dog hit him hard, a flurry of snapping white teeth and claws. Gabe lurched back as its jaws locked around his arm and bit uselessly into the suit. Flinging his arm as wide as possible, he sent the Alsatian skidding across the room. A second dog bolted through the door on the far side of the room, fangs bared, even as the one Gabe had thrown off wheeled round, coming back at him….

On instinct he slammed his hand down on the control hub. The Mosquito triggered and the dogs yelped in shock and pain, stopping short in their approach. In the chair, unable to cover his ears, Iain was crying out as well.

Suddenly, a burly guy flew at Gabe from the direction of the door – in his mid-thirties and oblivious to the noise. As the man threw an iron fist, Gabe raised his right arm. It glanced off the metal reinforcement built into the suit's forearm, but it didn't stop his attacker, who swung low with his left fist. It connected with the Mosquito by chance, killing the sound.

The dogs were immediately on the move again… but stopped short as a projectile exploded on the floor between them. They all looked up and saw Cathy with another roof tile in her hand, ready to fling it in their direction.

"The dogs!" she warned as she slung the tile. This time the man had to duck, as it whizzed overhead. Gabe saw both Alsatians coming at him at once, and decided that it was time to regroup.

Turning, he threw himself at the nearest window.

The suit carried him through, shards of glass bouncing off harmlessly. For a terrifying moment he was in free fall… before he smashed on to another sloping roof and began to tumble. Throwing out a hand, he caught the gutter, stopping his descent.

Dangling, he heard men's voices shouting from within the factory and from below. The barks of the dogs receded as they were ordered to find him.

And then, from the direction of the roof above, he heard a girl's cry. He didn't need the triumphant shout of one of the kidnappers to know that Cathy had been captured. A sudden silence fell over the complex as Gabe hung in the shadows. Before he could think about his options, the voice of a man came through a loudhailer from the rooftops above.

"Hello, hello, wherever you are." That voice had a mocking, almost amused tone to it. "I'm addressing our local superhero somewhere below me. My men are coming for you. Please be sensible and give yourself up and we can get this all sorted out.... I'm going to count to five.

One… Two… Three… Four…"

Gabe cursed inwardly, wishing that he'd done more to stop Cathy following him. Gritting his teeth and tensing for action, he made his choice….

Chapter 3

Shadow Warrior

Hanging off the side of the building as his enemies closed in, Gabe knew what he had to do. And it didn't involve giving himself up.

Releasing his grip on the gutter, he fell three metres to the ground, landing almost silently in the shadows by the wall. He waited there a moment, assessing his options.

Boot-steps were approaching from both left and right along the building. His pursuers were closing in. Directly ahead was open ground leading to the perimeter fence and escape from the complex. But that way was exposed… and more importantly the bad guys had Cathy. By the time he went for help and got back,

who knew what might have become of her…
and Iain?

You're the Guardian Angel, Gabe reminded himself. *It's up to you to save them.*

Spying a set of steps leading down to a basement door, a plan began to form in Gabe's mind. He'd take to the shadows inside the factory. Use his skills to evade and intimidate his pursuers. Show them what the Guardian Angel was all about.

He moved fast and low down the steps, but found the door secured with a heavy padlock. Above, the footsteps were getting closer and he could hear murmuring voices. They were clearly trying to be stealthy… but not doing a very good job of it.

Gabe reached for the mini-crowbar from his utility belt and weighed it in his gloved hand. This was going to create some noise, no doubt about it, but he had to get back inside the factory as soon as possible. Gabe knew he was outnumbered, maybe four or more to one, but inside the decaying building he could even the odds.

Placing the crowbar under the latch, he pulled down with all his strength.

SCREEEEECH!

The padlock and latch flew off. Men's voices yelled as Gabe yanked open the door and threw himself into the darkness beyond.

He found himself in a narrow passageway stretching ahead. No exits led off, so there was no choice but to go forward. Behind him the door opened and there was more yelling as several guys tried to squeeze through at once.

The corridor turned sharply up ahead. Gabe pulled a ping-pong ball from his belt and threw it behind him as he took the corner. A second later the homemade flash-bang went off, creating a brilliant light and bringing cries of confusion from his pursuers.

Knowing that the blinding flash would buy him roughly five seconds of time, Gabe put his head down and sprinted forward. The corridor widened out into a larger area – some kind of electrical systems room located in the basement level. Rows of old-fashioned control devices. Pipes and wires criss-crossed the ceiling. There were three exits leading off to different areas under the factory.

The footsteps started after him again. Gabe jumped, caught an overhead pipe in both hands and hauled himself up. Lying flat against the pipework, the darkness of his supersuit provided natural camouflage. Seconds later, his pursuers appeared below, looking disorientated as they peered at the various exits leading off the room.

One of the men reached for a radio and Gabe touched the control hub on his wrist, activating the communications scanner.

"Craven," the man barked into the radio. "We lost him."

Gabe grinned as the scanner locked on to the radio channel they were using, instantly patching him in so he could eavesdrop on both sides of the conversation.

"How could you lose him, Tony?" was the reply, heard by Gabe through the ear buds built into his helmet. He recognized the voice – it was the same person who had used the loudhailer earlier. Craven must be the gang leader.

"It's a maze down here!"

"Then split up and find him! He must *not* get out of the complex. Do you understand?"

The radio went dead before Tony could reply. As the henchmen grumbled among themselves and debated how to search the area, Gabe silently snapped pictures of their faces.

The collection of mugshots was less than pretty – the general look was crew-cuts and mean expressions – but it would be very good as evidence…. *If I ever get out of here*, Gabe thought ruefully. He wanted to text the pics directly through to the police, but the factory was built in a valley – a dead spot for mobile reception.

Finally, the henchmen left one guy covering the entrance, while the other three split up and headed deeper into the basement. They moved out more cautiously this time, clearly not comfortable in this part of the complex.

Just how I want it, thought Gabe.

He followed Tony, the one who'd spoken into the radio. A huge guy in combat gear with tattoos up both arms, he had a heavy-duty security torch that looked like a club clenched in one meaty fist.

Keeping to the overhead pipes, Gabe tailed him into another, larger, room. Tony shone his torch around an expanse of rotting cardboard boxes and rusting oil drums. The smell of petrol and oil was thick in the air.

"What a dump," Tony muttered.

"IT'S NOT SO BAD, TONY," Gabe said, giving him the full benefit of the Angel's vocal synth.

Tony's shocked face twisted up to where Gabe was crouched above him… as Gabe threw a smoke bomb at the man's feet. It exploded on impact and Tony staggered back, coughing and spluttering as the smoke enveloped him.

Gabe leaped down from the pipes and ran back the way he had come. Through his helmet com he heard Tony warning the others that he was headed in their direction.

Dashing through the control room, he took a corridor to the left – and ran into another henchman. Gabe went low, hitting the thug in the knees with his reinforced boots. Carried by his own weight, the man flew over Gabe's head and hit the wall with a thud.

"Baz, I'm coming!" yelled the third gang member, approaching from the direction of the control room.

Gabe opened a pocket on his belt and extracted a fistful of ball bearings. As the man barrelled into the corridor, Gabe threw them across the floor. The burly man skidded on them, lost his footing and hit the ground hard with a yelp of pain.

"There he is!" Tony's voice cried as he brought up the rear, huffing and puffing with exertion. He was a big man, and clearly out of shape.

Gabe threw another flash-bang down the corridor, along with a smoke bomb for good measure. Blinded and choking, his pursuers fell back.

Using the smoke cloud to mask his escape, Gabe slipped into the darkness again. He listened to the conversation that ensued over the radio.... This time he noted with satisfaction a new tone to the men's voices.

Fear.

"Craven!" Tony snapped. "We're getting messed up down here! He's got... weapons! And he... he knows our names!"

"He's hacked our coms, you idiot!" Craven's voice snapped back. "Get back here and keep radio silence until I say otherwise."

"But–"

"Radio SILENCE!" Craven snapped. "I'll deal with this guy myself."

The radio went dead. Tony gave his companions an angry order and they moved out.

Crouched in the shadows, Gabe listened as silence returned to the factory basement. All he could hear was the beating of his heart after the exertion of taking on four of Craven's henchmen… and beating them.

Round one to me, he thought elatedly.

"Hello?" It was Craven's voice on the radio channel. Gabe gave no response, although the mic in his helmet would have allowed it. "I'd like to speak to the little rat running around the basement, causing mischief. Speak up! Or are you afraid to talk?"

Gabe hesitated just a second, before responding in his Angel-synthesised voice, "HELLO… CRAVEN."

The man chuckled humourlessly over the radio. "So, you know my name. But I don't know yours."

Gabe didn't answer that one, deciding that the less he revealed at this stage, the better. Craven would learn about the Guardian Angel soon enough. Instead he said, "LET MY FRIENDS GO. LEAVE WHILE YOU STILL CAN."

Craven chuckled at that. "Well, you're obviously not a cop. They know better than to come around here and threaten me. And you've got some skills, I'll give you that. At least enough to put the wind up the morons who work for me." A pause. "But perhaps you'd like to speak to your friends. They're right here. Say hello… Cathy."

Silence.

Craven's voice roared, "Say hello!" There was the sound of something being smashed. Cathy screamed.

Gabe tensed, his gloved hands balling into fists. "LET HER GO."

"Make me! I'm on the top level of the main factory building." Craven's voice took on a mocking, sing-song quality. "I'll be waiting!"

The radio went dead. Gabe let out a slow breath. The gauntlet had been thrown down.

Chapter 4

Trapped!

An explosion momentarily lit up the night. The burning oil barrel rolled down the loading ramp at the side of the abandoned storage building to the north of the complex. As it hit a wall it had ruptured, sending a plume of fiery smoke into the air. The bang was satisfyingly loud as well.

Gabe kicked over another barrel and sent it careening down the ramp after the first. He'd found the barrels in the basement area and it had been easy enough to rig a lit fuse with a piece of rag and his mini-blowtorch.

He was almost halfway up the drainpipe leading to the top of the building when the second barrel went up. Light flashed in the corner of his vision, but he didn't slow, reaching the roof and pulling himself over into cover.

Then he waited.

It didn't take long for Craven's men to come running. He heard their confused shouting over the radios first, despite their leader's previous command to keep radio silence. Then he saw them running around below, trying to find some way to put out the fire. Time to move.

Gabe leaped across the rooftops until he landed on the sloping tiles of the factory where he'd first seen Iain. The skylight was open with the grappling hook still attached from where he'd entered before.

Reaching it, Gabe looked down and saw that Cathy was now tied to a chair beside Iain. There was no sign of any men below. His diversion had done the trick, it seemed. If Craven was around… he was nowhere to be seen.

But as Gabe tested the grapple and swung his body over the edge of the skylight, he had an uncomfortable thought. *This is too easy. Waaaay too easy.* But it was also his best chance to free the hostages and he had to take it.

Fighting down his pang of fear, Gabe slid smoothly down the rope and touched the ground, this time barely disturbing the dusty floorboards as he did so. He moved to Cathy's side and pulled a gag out of her mouth.

"What are you doing here?" she demanded, eyes flashing with anger.

"I'm saving you!"

Cathy rolled her eyes. "Idiot! Can't you see it's a trap!"

"Who is this clown, Cathy?" Iain demanded, craning his head round so he could see what was going on.

Gabe clenched his teeth, starting to untie Cathy's wrists. "Let's just focus on getting out of here…"

"The floor!" warned Cathy.

Gabe looked down and realized they were standing on a trapdoor a split second before…

…the floor dropped away under their feet.

They fell, but not far, crashing down into the room below. The chair to which Cathy was tied splintered and cracked and she rolled to one side. Iain landed beside her, yelling out in pain.

Gabe's fall was broken by the padding of his supersuit, but as he tried to scramble to his feet something heavy and clinging fell over him. He twisted around and immediately his arms became constricted. He was caught in a piece of heavy cargo netting, and the more he struggled the more tangled he became.

Keeping his head, he reached for the blowtorch from his belt with the intention of burning his way through the net… as the thickset shape of a man stepped out of the darkness. Something hit Gabe hard across the back of his knees and he went down again. A second man stepped in, making a grab at his arms.

In desperation, Gabe rolled himself away from his attackers, trying to reach another flash-bang on his belt. *Got to get the upper hand again*, he thought. But it was too late. Tony threw himself across Gabe's chest, pinning him to the floor. *Ooof!* The breath was knocked from his body.

The men dragged him up and held him tight as the net was pulled away. Lights flashed on, revealing a small room and the open trapdoor above them – clearly at some time it had been used as part of the factory production process. Cathy and Iain were lying on the floor, looking stunned but unhurt. Twisting his head, Gabe counted all four henchmen.

Then a voice Gabe recognized as that of Craven spoke up from the far side of the room. "Well, well. It seems there really is more than one way to catch a rat."

The henchmen holding Gabe turned him so he was facing their boss. Craven was slightly built in comparison to his gang members, who looked like a bunch of off-duty wrestlers, but he still possessed a wiry-looking strength. His eyes were intelligent, almost sensitive, but his thin lips were locked in what appeared to be a permanent sneer. He took in the sight of the

Guardian Angel with barely a blink of his eyes.

"That's a very unusual look you have there," he said finally.

"Let's see this guy's face," said Tony, who was holding Gabe's right arm. He reached to tear off the helmet.

"No!" Craven held up a finger as if he'd just been struck by a brilliant idea. "Leave it on!"

The henchmen looked at one another questioningly as Craven approached. He clapped his hands together with apparent glee, looking Gabe up and down. "Can't you see it's perfect? My very own superhero! Every great villain needs a great crime-fighting opponent. And it looks as if I've just found mine – straight out of a comic book!"

"It's just a bloke in a wetsuit, boss," said the henchman on Gabe's left arm. "Look. This stuff is all homemade."

He plucked a canister from Gabe's utility belt and started trying to twist the top off.

"I WOULDN'T DO THAT," warned Gabe.

"Shut up, loser," the thug snapped… as the lid came off the pepper-spray bomb. "AAAARGH!" He staggered back, clutching at his face.

"TOLD YOU," said Gabe as another man stepped up, roughly taking hold of his arm.

"Nice," said Craven, nodding his approval and looking around the increasingly confused faces of his men. "How many times have I told you guys that a life of crime isn't just about the money?" He sighed in frustration when there was no response. "What is it also about?"

The henchmen answered together, rather unenthusiastically. "The kicks."

"That's right. The kicks."

Craven rounded on Gabe, smiling maliciously. "Keep your mask and your weapons. Let's find out if you're worthy to be my nemesis."

"WHAT DO YOU HAVE IN MIND?" asked Gabe, thinking that he probably wasn't going to like the answer. Craven was clearly insane. Scary. Unpredictable. He sensed that even Craven's men, who came across as a bunch of hardened criminals, were scared of him.

"A test," said Craven, grabbing Cathy's arm and dragging her up in front of Gabe. "A little test of your…er…powers. How do you fancy that, superhero?"

"He's called the Guardian Angel," snapped Cathy, struggling against Craven's grasp. "And he's not going to play your stupid game."

Craven grinned at her. "Oh, I think he will. I need Iain for the ransom money from his rich daddy. But I don't need you two." He looked from Cathy to Gabe, an eyebrow raised. "Get it?"

"YES," Gabe replied. The threat was clear enough. "I GET IT."

Tony stepped closer to Craven so he could whisper in his ear. "C'mon, boss. Let's just lock him in the basement. We don't need this."

Craven's head jerked round, eyes flashing anger. "*The kicks!*" he spat.

Tony stepped back swiftly.

Craven turned slowly to Gabe. "Pass my little test, and you can both go free. Fail and… you'll see." An icy smile passed across his smirking lips. "Now, step this way…."

Chapter 5

Tried and Tested

Even through his supersuit, the night air had a biting chill to it as Gabe stepped off the access ladder and on to the rooftop. Tony came up immediately behind him, pushing him roughly as the others followed.

The building on which they stood was five storeys high, the tallest in the factory. Looking across the complex, Gabe saw three brick chimneys rising – at one time they would have belched smoke into the atmosphere twenty-four hours a day, but now they were disused, like everything else. With his keen vision, Gabe made out a thick telephone cable stretching from the top of the building to the midpoint of the nearest chimney. It then passed on to a second chimney and a smaller third chimney in the distance.

So that's it, thought Gabe grimly. He could guess what Craven had in mind.

"Move," ordered Tony, jabbing him in the back with a thick finger. Gabe turned and almost knocked the thug's hand away, but he saw Cathy being held fast by two more of the henchmen and knew he had no choice. He stepped towards the edge of the roof.

A roof tile dropped from the building. It had been tossed by Craven, who appeared at his side. The tile shattered against the concrete far below.

"That's a long drop!" Craven said with a wince. "I hope you have a good head for heights, hero."

"LET'S GET ON WITH IT," hissed Gabe.

"A man of action! I like that!" Craven pointed across the complex, tracing the line of high wires between the chimneys. "These old telephone cables stretch right to the other side of the factory. They *should* be strong enough to take the weight of a person… hopefully." That got a laugh from his men. "All you have to do is walk the cables to the farthest chimney."

Gabe looked at him. "AND IF I REACH IT, YOU'LL LET CATHY AND ME GO?"

"That's what I said, didn't I?" snapped Craven, his voice taking on a dangerous tone. "Don't you trust me?

"I DON'T HAVE MUCH CHOICE, DO I?"

Craven grinned. "Not really." He gestured to the wire. "Ready when you are."

Gabe took a deep breath and placed his right foot on the cable….

"Don't do it!" Cathy's voice rang out before a henchman clamped a hand over her mouth.

"IT'S GOING TO BE OKAY," said Gabe, glancing at her. Then he turned his attention back to the wire, testing his weight against it. It was taut and seemed firm enough. The cable itself was thick, making it easier to balance on the soles of his boots. All he had to do was try to forget the drop… five storeys straight down.

With a deep breath, Gabe stepped fully on to the cable and balanced there for a moment, throwing out his arms for stability. A sudden gust of wind rocked him, but he was ready for that, shifting his weight to maintain balance.

"Get going," said Tony, about to jab him in the back again.

Gabe moved before the thug made contact – two quick, even steps out on to the wire, his feet angled to achieve maximum stability. He took another breath… fixed his gaze on the chimney, his goal… and took two more steps… then two more.

This brought him roughly a third of the way across the cable and he stopped as another gust of wind howled through the complex. *Just keep breathing*, he told himself. *Keep your eyes dead ahead.* The urge to look down was almost overpowering. But Gabe knew that seeing the chasm beneath wouldn't do his balance any good.

Craven's voice floated across the gap between the buildings. "You done this before, Guardian Angel?"

Gabe smiled behind his mask. *Wouldn't you like to know?* In fact, as part of his training to become the Guardian Angel, he'd worked extensively on his balance. It was an essential skill in freerunning, which he'd practised at night around town – leaping across walls and rooftops. And there was the tightrope he'd strung between the garage and the back fence. But, of course, that was only a couple of metres off the ground, not several storeys…

Don't think about the drop, Gabe ordered himself. *It's just another rope walk.*

He kept going. Two more steps. And then another two. Arms out for balance. Breathing steady. With another couple of steps he was over halfway across and the side of the chimney seemed almost within reach. His heart beat faster… *I can do this.*

"He's gonna make it!" exclaimed Tony, his voice a mix of surprise and disappointment.

"We'll see about that," replied Craven. "Hey, Angel!"

Against his better judgement, Gabe looked over his shoulder. Craven was crouching by the edge of the roof. There was a knife in his hand now.

"Remember how I said you could trust me?" Craven placed the blade against the telephone cable. "I lied."

He slashed the wire….

Gabe was already throwing himself forward, reaching out as the cable lost tension beneath him. He caught it in his gloved hands as it fell away. For a second he was in free fall, then the wire went taut so violently that he was almost wrenched free. But Gabe held firm, swinging hard and fast towards the side of the chimney.

He slammed against the brickwork with enough force to knock the air from his body, although the padding of his suit absorbed much of the blow. His arms felt as if they were ready to fall out of their sockets, but he forced himself to start climbing the dangling section of telephone cable. Using the tips of his boots for purchase, he climbed the remaining distance to the top of the chimney where the second cable was attached. Here he rested a moment, clinging on to the gaps between the bricks.

"Impressive!" Craven's voice echoed across the complex. Gabe saw the gang leader glaring across at him. "I can hardly believe it."

"YOU CHEATED!" Gabe called back. "*THAT'S* NO SURPRISE."

Craven shrugged. "I just want to make it interesting for you – keep you on your toes!" He turned to two of his men and gave an order that was impossible to hear. As they moved out of view, Craven looked back at Gabe. "Okay, so I bent the rules a little! If you carry on, I won't lift a finger against you." He made a *cross-my-heart-and-hope-to-die* motion across his chest with the knife. "Promise."

Gabe gritted his teeth, giving no response. What choice did he have? Craven had Cathy and all he could do was play out the madman's game to the bitter end….

He turned his attention to the next section of cable, which stretched ahead to the midpoint of the next chimney. This gap was a little shorter, maybe only fifteen metres, but Gabe was exhausted from his previous effort. *Got to keep going. At least Craven can't cut the cable this time.* He took several deep breaths before stepping out.

He made it halfway across before the first projectile hit him… something hard and blunt-edged colliding with his left shoulder. The force of the blow almost sent him tumbling, but with flailing arms, Gabe managed to keep his balance. A second object flew by, narrowly missing him.

Gabe looked in the direction from which the object had come. One of Craven's henchmen was standing on a rooftop below with another tile in his hand. He hurled this at Gabe, who leaned left just a little so it sailed on by.

"Now, I promised that I wouldn't sabotage you," Craven's voice echoed eerily off the surrounding buildings. "But I can't speak for my men." A maniacal laugh pierced the air.

Without looking back, Gabe forged on, walking the cable as fast as he dared. This was at the expense of his balance, so when another tile bounced off the side of his helmet he almost went down…. The henchman gave a whoop of triumph and hurled yet another tile. This time Gabe was ready. He shot out a hand and caught it in mid-air, and then sent it flying back in the direction it had come. The tile exploded at the feet of the thug, shattering the tiles beneath. The man lost his balance on the sloped roof and went sliding down to the gutter.

Not wasting a second, Gabe crossed the final metres to the side of the second chimney, pressing himself to the bricks.

The next cable stretched down towards the shorter, third chimney – and this downward slope was going to make walking it very difficult. Voices below reminded him that the bad guys were closing in – who knew what they'd try next. Unclipping his utility belt, Gabe looped it over the last cable and took a tight grip of each end. *Let's do this the fast way*, he thought as he leaped off the edge of the chimney.

Holding the belt as if he was on a zip wire, Gabe whizzed the length of the cable in seconds. As the chimney approached, he put out his boots to stop from crashing into it. Finally he pulled himself on to the top of the structure.

"HEY, CRAVEN!" he called across the complex. "I MADE IT! LET THE GIRL GO!"

"You haven't made it yet, mate," said a voice near his feet.

Gabe looked round in time to see one of the henchmen at the top of a ladder running up the side of the chimney. He had a length of wood in his hands, which he swung at the back of Gabe's knees. His legs buckled under him and then he was falling towards the mouth of the chimney….

Gabe let out a cry and was swallowed by the total darkness….

Chapter 6

"He's finished"

"What happened?" Craven demanded impatiently over the radio.

"I knocked him into the chimney," replied the henchman. "He's finished."

Craven made a growling sound. "I'll believe that when I see the body."

The henchman sounded confused. "It's… uh… dark down there. But no way did he survive–"

"I want proof!" Craven yelled. "All of you. Search the area and find him – dead or alive! This isn't over until I have the Guardian Angel in front of me!"

The radio clicked to silence.

Hanging by the very tips of his fingers from a ledge halfway up the inside of the chimney, Gabe had listened to the exchange via his helmet com. They thought they'd beaten him… or at least the henchmen did. That gave him the advantage. His eyes were already adjusting to the darkness of the chimney and he made out a series of raised bricks in the surface of the wall. These formed a kind of ladder– perhaps used for maintenance in the past.

Swinging his legs, Gabe leaped to the first brick and from there it was easy enough to climb down to the very bottom of the chimney. This was a wide, circular area clogged with ancient soot. Gabe kicked open an access door and found himself in the basement area once more – this time in the furnace rooms. And by his estimation practically right next door to the building where they were keeping Iain.

He sprinted through the narrow corridors, ignoring the fatigue in his aching limbs. *When this is all over*, he thought, *I'll sleep for a week.*

But for now I've got work to do. Nobody said being the Guardian Angel was going to be easy.

Craven had left just one of his men guarding Iain… and not his best man either. As Gabe slipped up into the top level, he found Iain once more tied to the chair above the trapdoor. The guard was seated opposite, dozing, his head lolling against his chest.

A wolfish howl echoed from the depths of the building and Gabe tensed, expecting to hear the sound of claws on the floorboards – but it seemed that Craven's attack dogs had been locked up for now.

Iain had the good sense to keep quiet as Gabe sneaked up on the henchman and pulled his arms behind the chair, quickly securing his wrists with a cable tie from his belt. By the time the guard was fully awake, Gabe had his ankles fastened to the legs of the chair as well. He stuffed a rag in the man's mouth before he could call out, then kicked the chair backwards. The man landed on his back with a muffled cry.

Gabe moved to Iain and released his bonds with a cutting tool.

Iain looked at him with wide, terrified eyes. "We have to run!" He grabbed Gabe's arm. "I don't know who you are, but my dad is *very* rich. Get me out of here now and you'll be well rewarded…."

Gabe pulled his arm free and pressed his helmet visor close to Iain's face. The other boy shrank back. "CRAVEN STILL HAS CATHY. WE'RE NOT LEAVING WITHOUT HER!"

"But these men are dangerous," Iain whimpered.

"WHICH IS WHY WE WON'T LEAVE CATHY WITH THEM!" Gabe growled. "SHE ONLY GOT INTO THIS MESS BECAUSE SHE WANTED TO HELP *YOU!* GOT IT?"

Iain nodded frantically. Gabe pulled an object that looked like a looped piece of netting from a compartment in the back of his suit.

"What are you going to do?" asked Iain as he watched Gabe spread out the loop on the floor and then cover it with dust as best he could.

"CRAVEN'S COMING," Gabe replied without looking up. "AND THIS TIME I'LL BE READY FOR HIM."

They didn't have to wait long. Craven appeared without his men, holding Cathy by the arm. With a disgusted look at his henchman bound to the chair, he turned his attention to the Guardian Angel standing in the middle of the room. Iain hovered in the shadows.

"I knew I hadn't seen the last of you," Craven said, studying Gabe with his gaze. "Technically, using that last cable as a zip-line is cheating… but I won't hold it against you."

Gabe folded his arms across his chest, saying nothing.

"What have you done with my prisoner?" Craven demanded, signalling to the empty chair in the middle of the room.

Gabe simply shrugged.

"I'll do you a trade," said Craven. "The girl for the rich kid. I only really care about the money, after all."

"SORRY, CRAVEN," said Gabe, "NO MORE GAMES. YOU DON'T PLAY FAIR."

Craven took on a mock expression of shock. "That hurts me! It really does!" He pushed Cathy to one side. The knife appeared in his hand and he grinned maniacally. "Let's just fight each other then."

"FINE WITH ME." Gabe signalled to Cathy to keep back as Craven moved in. They circled around the room, Gabe keeping a close watch on his opponent's position.

"What are you waiting for?" demanded Craven, tensed for an attack.

"FOR YOU TO BE STANDING RIGHT THERE." Gabe tapped the control screen on his wrist…

…the shape charge he'd laid on the floor detonated in wide circle around Craven – like a series of firecrackers going off. The explosion was powerful enough to cut a hole right through the decaying boards. A section of floor dropped away under Craven's feet and he disappeared with a cry… and then a dull thud from below.

"LET'S MOVE!" Gabe ordered, already running for the door. Cathy and Iain were hot on his heels.

They fled through the building. There was no sign of Craven's men, but Gabe knew they couldn't be far away. At the ground level entrance he signalled Cathy and Iain to stop and they crouched in the shadows.

"What was that back there?" whispered Cathy.

"Homemade explosives," replied Gabe, modulating his Guardian Angel voice to a lower volume.

Iain laughed incredulously. "You carry explosives around in your backpack?" But when Cathy shot him a look, he added, "Hey, thanks for rescuing me back there."

"We need to get out of here," Gabe said.

"When Craven had me up on the rooftops I had the chance to have a good look around," Cathy said. "I think our best bet is to steal one of their vehicles and smash our way out. There are some trucks parked on the south side. We could use one to break through the outer fence."

Chapter 7

Breakout!

Gabe, Cathy and Iain crouched beside a pile of wooden pallets in the warehouse area of the factory. An articulated truck stood a few metres away, while a single henchman patrolled the area. In one hand he held a torch. In the other, a leash with two of Craven's attack dogs on the end.

"That's how we're getting out of here," whispered Gabe, pointing at the truck.

Iain made a muffled snorting sound. "In that piece of junk? So much for a fast getaway!"

Gabe looked at him. "Got a better idea?"

Cathy put herself between them. "If you two could stop bickering for a moment, there's the small matter of the henchman and those Alsatians?"

"I'll handle it," said Gabe, leaping over the pallets before they could argue. "Cover your ears." He moved swiftly and silently along the loading ramp.

The dogs growled and strained against the leash, sensing his approach. The henchman pulled them back with a curse. Gabe reached to his belt and activated his trusty Mosquito with immediate effect. The guard dogs went crazy as the high-pitched wail hit them. This time they tore the leash completely free of the henchman's grasp. When he tried to grab one of the dogs it turned on him, sinking its teeth into his wrist.

"Aaargh!" yelled the thug. The dogs fled whimpering into the depths of the factory and the henchmen tore off in pursuit, cradling his hand.

As Cathy and Iain ran from their hiding place, Gabe killed the Mosquito and pointed to the truck, indicating they should get inside.

Gabe seated himself behind the wheel, with Cathy beside him. "Let's go!" he cried.

"Great plan," said Iain as he ran to the other door and climbed inside. "No keys."

"Who needs them?" said Gabe. Ripping the plastic casing off the steering column, he exposed the wires inside. Gabe pulled a couple loose and touched the ends together as he pumped the accelerator pedal. The windscreen wipers came on.

"Argh, wrong ones," Gabe growled. He tried two different wires. The truck engine turned over once and died.

At the far end of the cargo bay there was the rumbling sound of a roller door opening.

"Hurry up!" cried Cathy, pointing ahead. More of Craven's men were running through the door towards them.

Gritting his teeth with concentration, Gabe touched the wires together… pumped the pedal… just right….

The truck engine roared into life.

"Hold on!" said Gabe, throwing the truck into gear and releasing the handbrake. The vehicle lurched forward, almost stalling. He floored the gas and the engine took. The truck started picking up speed as a henchman grabbed on to the passenger door.

"Get lost!" yelled Cathy, kicking open the door. The man went flying.

With a bit of effort, Gabe hit second gear and steered the truck down the loading ramp. It picked up speed on the slope. As it sped across a courtyard, he watched their pursuers recede in the side-view mirror.

"Look out!" cried Iain, pointing to the perimeter fence coming up fast.

But Gabe had no intention of stopping. He pressed his foot down, increasing speed.

The truck smashed through the chain-link fence, barely slowing, and juddered across the uneven ground surrounding the complex. Seeing a dirt track, Gabe steered in that direction. They were headed through the old quarries, a maze of dust roads and canyons left over from Estruca's industrial past.

"I can't believe we made it!" cried Iain, suddenly elated, punching the roof of the cab with his fist. Staring at Gabe, he said, "You might look like a freak, but I have to admit… you've got skills."

"Thanks," replied Gabe, clenching his jaw.

"Now take me home," Iain ordered.

Gabe shook his head as he steered the truck round a tight bend. "We're going to the police. Craven has to be stopped."

"*The cops*!" exclaimed Iain. "They know exactly what Craven's up to out here! Why do you think they haven't arrested him before now?"

"You're saying the police are in on this?" asked Gabe.

"Craven *owns* them," Iain snapped back. He looked at Cathy. "Tell him!"

Cathy shrugged when he turned to her. "My dad's got some… concerns. He thinks there might be corruption–"

"I've been missing for over a week," Iain pointed out, interrupting Cathy. "And *you* managed to find me. Do you think the cops have really been…"

His voice trailed away as lights appeared on the track behind them. Gabe checked the mirror and made out three vehicles – two dirt bikes and a pickup – approaching fast. Craven's men were in pursuit!

As one of the dirt bikes roared up their right-hand side, Gabe swung the wheel, sending the truck towards it. But the rider anticipated the move and zipped away over the rough ground at the side of the road. The second bike came up the other side and Gabe saw the man reaching for the side of the truck….

He slammed on the brakes and the bike shot ahead. Gabe stepped on the gas again and the truck continued labouring along the road.

"This isn't working!" cried Cathy. "They're too fast!"

One of the bikes came back in and this time the rider managed to grab on to the back of the truck. In the mirror, Gabe saw the bike go tumbling away as the henchman clung on to the vehicle, moving towards the front.

"These guys don't give up!" exclaimed Iain.

"Take the wheel," said Gabe, moving to one side so Cathy could take his seat. "I'm going to shake them off."

"But I can't drive!" Cathy protested as Gabe opened the cab door and started out.

Neither can I, Gabe thought to himself. "Just stay in second gear and keep your foot on the gas – no matter what!" he called back.

Clinging fast to the truck against the wind rushing past, he moved round to the back of the cab where it joined the trailer. A sign on the coupling read, *TRAILER RELEASE WARNING: DO NOT ATTEMPT WHILE VEHICLE IS IN MOTION*. Gabe had an idea. If he could get rid of the trailer, the cab would be much faster and more manoeuvrable.

Without warning, the fist of a henchman connected with the side of Gabe's helmet, knocking him back against the wall of the cab.

The biker swung round from the side of the trailer. But as his opponent advanced, Gabe raised his left hand, fingers flexed up.… The release mechanism on the foam canister built into the arm of the supersuit triggered at the motion. Sticky foam squirted in the henchman's face. The man clawed at the liquid clinging to his skin.

"BYE," said Gabe, pushing him back. The henchman hit the soft ground at the side of the track and rolled away, dazed, into a ditch.

A thump from the truck body alerted him that another pursuer had jumped from his bike. Gabe went high, climbing on to the roof of the trailer. The henchman clearly had the same idea, because he appeared from the back. Gabe went into a crouch, throwing his arms out for balance as the truck took a corner too sharply and almost tipped over. Somehow Cathy managed to keep it on the road.

The henchman lurched forward, swinging wildly… but he was off balance. Gabe moved to one side and hit his shoulder, almost sending the man over the edge. But he held on and came round for another attack.

Gabe saw it before his opponent and ducked, just in time, as the low branch of a tree whipped over the roof of the cab and struck the henchman in the chest. He rolled off the truck, cursing as he landed in a shrub below.

WHAM!

The pickup hit the back of the trailer, almost jolting Gabe off the top. The entire truck careened to the left, in danger of running off the road once again.

"HOLD ON JUST A LITTLE LONGER!" Gabe yelled to Cathy, as he jumped down into the gap at the back of the cab once more.

"Make it fast!" Cathy called back as the truck was rammed again.

After a quick examination of the coupling rig, Gabe ripped the cables free and kicked the release lever. There was a terrific grinding sound as the trailer came free. Gabe leaped on to the back of the cab and clung on as the trailer fell away and collided with the speeding pickup. They crashed to a halt in the middle of the track and disappeared from view as the cab sped away.

Gabe climbed back through the door, taking the wheel from Cathy. "Nice driving," he said.

She grinned at him. "Nice job getting rid of the bad guys."

On the other side of the cab, Iain folded his arms across his chest grumpily. "If you've finished congratulating each other, perhaps you wouldn't mind taking me home?"

Cathy rolled her eyes, but leaned in to whisper to Gabe, "If we can't trust the Estruca police force, Big George is probably the only person we can go to for help with this."

Gabe knew she had a point and acknowledged it with a nod. As the truck came to the end of the dirt track, he swung it in the direction of Iain's home. Of course, everyone in Estruca knew where Big George Thompson lived – the mansion on the hill, a constant reminder that he was the richest man in town.

It took less than five minutes to reach the part of Estruca where the mansion was located, the truck making much better progress on the tarmacked road. The entrance to Thompson Towers (as the building was jokingly known) was guarded by two wrought iron gates at the end of a long, rising drive.

Iain started saying, "I'll call the guard to open…"

Gabe gunned the engine and sent the truck smashing through the gates at high speed. Iain gave him a murderous look. "Sorry," said Gabe, grinning behind his mask. "I just wanted to get you home as *quickly* as possible."

He pulled the truck up sharply in front of the mansion and they all jumped out.

"Where's the security?" said Iain, looking around the darkened house. "My dad usually has guards posted around the estate 24/7."

Great, thought Gabe, *rich and paranoid….
Obviously with good reason, though, I guess.*

"Let's just get inside," Cathy said, nervously eyeing the road behind them as if expecting to see Craven's men in pursuit at any moment.

Gabe laid a reassuring hand on her shoulder. "It's okay. We lost them."

She smiled and nodded. They ran up the steps to the mansion door and found it open.

Chapter 8

Big George

The entrance hall to Thompson Towers was lined in marble, with twin staircases curving up to the first floor. Ahead, on the ground floor, double doors were open, revealing a massive formal dining room beyond – and it was from here that Iain's father appeared.

Big George Thompson lived up to his name. He was well over six feet tall and almost as wide, his gut straining against the buttons of his shirt. Yet for all his weight, he seemed to glide across the glistening tiles towards them, crocodile-skin shoes making no sound as he approached.

"Son!" Big George exclaimed, his dark, button-like eyes widening. He rushed forward and threw his thick arms around Iain, who returned the embrace awkwardly. "Did they hurt you?"

Iain started babbling, "They tied me up and it was cold and there was no Internet and…." His voice trailed away as he thought of something. "Why didn't you pay the kidnappers, Daddy?"

Big George gave his son a reproachful look. "You know that this was a complicated situation…. Many… uh… variables…." He looked to Gabe and Cathy, as if noticing them for the first time. One eyebrow rose at the sight of Gabe's supersuit. "And who are you?"

"Oh, they helped me break out of the factory," Iain said. "But, Daddy, I want to know–"

"Well, I owe you both a great debt," said Big George, stepping in front of his son. "Let me shake your hand…."

He raised his right arm, as if in greeting. Too late, Gabe realized that there was something clasped in those pudgy fingers….

Big George jabbed a Taser hard into Gabe's side, two metal pins piercing the supersuit to his skin. Electricity crackled and Gabe felt as if he'd been hit with a sledgehammer. His body jerked and flew back hard.

He was unconscious before he hit the marble floor….

* * *

"Wake up! Angel! Wake up!"

At the sound of Cathy's voice, Gabe raised his head, although it felt as if there was a weight pressing down on his skull. The blast from the stun gun had left his muscles aching. He tried to move and found his arms and legs secured to a chair. Cathy was tied up behind him.

Big George appeared down the stairway, a suitcase in each hand. "You're awake," he said. "Sorry about all this."

Gabe raised his head and asked, "WHAT'S GOING ON?"

Big George considered for a moment. "Just before you arrived Craven called me with a deal that I couldn't refuse. It seems he wants *you* even more badly than he wants my money, *Guardian Angel*."

"SO, YOU DO KNOW HIM."

Big George nodded. "Craven was an employee of mine back in the days when I was making my fortune. He was useful – a man who wasn't afraid to get his hands dirty. Of course, I soon realized he was insane. I tried to get rid of him, and he took it… badly."

"SO HE KIDNAPPED YOUR SON," growled Gabe.

"You can understand why I couldn't go to the police," said Big George. "Craven's a mad dog that turned on his master – he knows some of my darkest secrets…." He placed a briefcase at Gabe's feet. "There's a million dollars in there. Tell Craven it's all his."

As Iain appeared from the direction of the dining room, his father tossed one of the suitcases at him. "We're leaving this cursed town for good." He looked around with apparent disgust and then headed towards the door.

"Come on, Iain!"

His son made to follow, then had a thought. Walking back to Gabe, he reached to rip off his mask....

"No!" cried Big George. "Craven wants him in the suit. That's the deal."

Iain's face fell, but then he grinned at Gabe. "Thanks for rescuing me… *Guardian Idiot*." He gave Gabe a mocking pat on the arm and trotted back to his father.

"Iain what are you *doing*?" yelled Cathy. "You can't leave us here. I risked everything to rescue you!"

"Sorry," Iain replied with a shrug.

"Let's go," growled Big George, pushing his son out of the door.

"I don't know who's worse," hissed Cathy as the pair left the mansion, "Iain or his father."

Gabe watched the front doors slam. "Oh, Iain's not so bad," he said, twisting the steak knife that the boy had secretly placed in his hand – a little act of gratitude for the rescue, it seemed. He pushed the blade against the rope holding his wrists and started to saw.

Cathy craned her head round to see what he was doing as Big George's car roared away from the house. Gabe kept working the ropes as new headlights appeared through the windows of the hallway.

"Craven's coming," she said.

"I know." With a grunt of effort, Gabe sawed through the final strand of rope and pulled his hands free. After untying his ankles, Gabe moved to free Cathy.

"I take it you have a plan?" she said as he untied her.

"Yeah," said Gabe, "Listen up…"

Chapter 9

Showdown

Craven pushed open the double doors to Thompson Towers and walked slowly across the marble hall, limping just slightly from his earlier fall. The mansion was silent, eerily so. In the middle of the hall stood two chairs, back to back, with severed pieces of rope on the floor beneath them. A leather briefcase rested on one of the chairs.

Looking left and right as he approached, Craven picked up the briefcase, weighed it in his hands and then flicked the catches. The case sprang open....

Empty.

Craven stared at the case for a few seconds....

Before smashing it against the marble floor with a yell that echoed throughout the deserted mansion.

"WHERE'S MY MONEY?" he screamed at the ceiling.

The house was silent.

Shaking his head, Craven began to chuckle, low and threatening. "I know you're still here, Angel!" he called. "You're not smart enough to run! Give me the cash and I'll let you and the girl go!"

Again silence. Craven picked up one of the chairs and threw it.

"ANGEL!"

There was a sudden blast of white noise as a hidden sound system sprang into life. Craven spun round, eyes wide, waiting.

"HELLO, CRAVEN," said the voice of the Guardian Angel, floating down from speakers high in the ceiling. "IF YOU WANT YOUR MONEY, YOU'LL HAVE TO PLAY A GAME. YOU LIKE GAMES, DON'T YOU?"

A grimace-like smile spread across Craven's face.

"HERE'S A RIDDLE," the Guardian Angel continued. "I HID THE FIRST STACK OF BILLS IN BIG GEORGE'S FAVOURITE ROOM IN THE HOUSE."

The man looked around and started towards the staircase….

"COLD," said the Guardian Angel.

Craven cursed… looked around… and then started across the hall….

"WARM."

Craven approached the open doorway to the dining room….

"WARMER!"

Seeing a stack of hundred-dollar bills lying on the dining room table directly ahead, Craven stepped through the doorway…

"RED HOT!"

…his foot caught the trip wire strung across the gap. A series of smoke bombs triggered, sending Craven staggering back, choking. With a cry of rage, he threw himself through the smoke, grabbed the money and ran back to the hall.

"WELL DONE," said the Angel. "WOULD YOU LIKE THE NEXT CLUE?"

Craven looked up at the CCTV camera and held up the wad of bills. Slowly and deliberately, he ripped the paper holding them together and threw the wad high.

For a moment the air was full of banknotes.

And when it cleared, Craven was gone.

* * *

"I think you annoyed him," said Cathy. She was sitting by Gabe's side in the security room of the mansion, located on the first floor of the east wing. A tablecloth with the rest of Big George's million dollars wrapped inside was at her feet. Before them was a bank of monitors, showing CCTV footage of parts of the building, inside and out. The one focused on the hallway showed no sign of Craven.

Gabe flicked the feed to the cameras in the adjoining rooms. A dark shape passed one and then was gone. Craven was on the move.

"I was hoping to keep him occupied a little longer," admitted Gabe. He looked at Cathy, who was on her mobile phone. "Any luck reaching your dad?"

She shook her head, hitting the speed dial number again. The phone rang with no answer. "I've left him a message, but he must be out on an operation," she said.

"Then it looks as if we're going to have to take on Craven ourselves," said Gabe, grimly. He'd already sent the pictures of Craven's gang to *whistleblower365*, his mystery contact. If he and Cathy didn't make it, at least there was a chance the gang would be brought to justice. But he was under no illusions – with half the local police in Craven's pay, they were on their own.

He turned his attention back to the screens, flicking through them quickly as he searched for his opponent. *He has to be somewhere.*

A deep rumbling sound started all around the mansion.

"What's that?" asked Cathy as the noise increased. To Gabe it sounded like a hundred garage roller-doors winding down at once.

"Look!" exclaimed Cathy, her sense of panic rising. Gabe glanced at the monitors. Metal security shutters were lowering across all of the external windows. Gabe flicked to the CCTV feed of the main entrance. It was now sealed by a steel gate. The mansion had been turned into an effective prison – there was no way in or out.

"Craven's found a way to tap into the security system," Gabe said, touching the override controls on the desk in front of him.

No use.

One by one, the CCTV monitors began to turn to static.

"We should get out of here," Cathy said quietly, picking up the bundle of money.

"Right," Gabe agreed. "It's the first place Craven will look."

They moved to the door, Gabe leading the way. He checked outside and, seeing no sign of Craven, moved down the plush carpeted corridor.

"Where are we heading?" whispered Cathy.

"There has to be a way out of here," said Gabe as they reached a landing between the east wing and the main house. The window here was firmly sealed by the security shutter. Gabe tried pulling it up, to no effect. It looked sturdy enough to withstand even a blast from a small explosive.

Cathy gave a small cry and placed a hand on Gabe's arm. He turned and saw their enemy standing on the other side of the landing.

Craven had been busy. He was now wearing a protective mask. A tank strapped was to his back. From it came a tube that ended in a long pipe with a trigger, which Craven cradled before him in both hands. A blue flame burned at the end of the pipe. Gabe clenched his jaw… Craven had a flamethrower.

"I helped Big George install the security system for this house," Craven gloated, approaching slowly. "I know all the overrides. This is my turf."

"Run," whispered Gabe.

Cathy looked as if she was about to argue, but Gabe pushed her away. She started sprinting down the corridor, the bundle of money swinging in her hand. Gabe turned slowly back to Craven, who smiled at him coldly.

"Alone at last," he said, adjusting the tank on his back and pointing the flamethrower nozzle at Gabe. "Given your love of gadgets, I thought you might like to see one of Big George's favourite toys. My old flamethrower." He looked at it lovingly. "Built it myself. Big George kept it locked in his basement, wouldn't let me have it after I… ahem… burned down a couple of houses."

"VERY NICE," hissed Gabe, tensing his legs, ready for action… because he knew what was coming next!

Craven pressed the trigger. A ten-metre long jet of fire shot from the flamethrower directly at Gabe…

…who was already moving for the edge of the landing. He grabbed the bannister rail and leaped over the side, feeling the heat as the flames swept towards him. He was saved by his suit. But as he landed on the floor below, he let out a cry of pain, his ankle twisting underneath him.

Above, Craven appeared at the bannister, aiming the flame gun down. Gabe somersaulted forward, crashing through a set of heavy double doors as fire exploded behind him. Ignoring the pain in his ankle, he moved swiftly into cover and crouched in the relative darkness of the room…and waited.

Chapter 10

"Time to leave"

Taking stock of his surroundings, Gabe saw that he was in the mansion's library. Shelves of leather-bound books ran from floor to ceiling. Above a fireplace hung a life-size portrait of Big George, sitting on a horse. A door on the far side of the room led somewhere… but that would mean crossing open ground. Footsteps approached and, looking round, Gabe saw Craven framed in the doorway.

"Ah, the library," he chuckled. "Just about the most flammable room in the house."

Gabe didn't breathe as Craven began to walk between the furniture arranged in the middle of the room.

"I know you're in here somewhere, Angel," he taunted. "You did a good job with my men, I have to admit. Now it's just you and me."

He passed by Gabe's hiding place and carried on towards the fireplace, stopping to look up at the portrait. "You know, I always wanted to do this. Bye Georgie."

He turned the flamethrower on the picture. In seconds it was a burning mass, Big George's image blackened to a crisp. The canvas disintegrated and fell off the wall.

Gabe exploded from his hiding place, sprinting for the door on the far side of the wall. Craven was already turning. His weapon spat fire once more. Rows of books burst into flame, a wave of heat following Gabe as he crashed into the adjoining room. It was a long room containing Big George's gallery of antique artefacts in neat, glass cases. A giant chandelier hung above the centre of the room, its crystals sparkling.

Gabe looked around wildly for a means of escape, but it seemed there was only one way in and out of the room. He was trapped. At the sound of Craven's footsteps behind him, he vaulted for the window, aiming a flying kick against the shutter.

Useless.

"No way out, Angel," said Craven as he stepped through the door, a plume of smoke from the burning library following him. He turned the flamethrower on the room and let rip…. Glass display cases shattered in the searing heat. Gabe pressed himself against the shutter, trying to keep away from the advancing wall of flame.

"Craven!" Cathy's voice rang out loud and clear, even over the roar of the flamethrower. Both Gabe and Craven turned to see her standing at the back of the gallery, one hand over her mouth against the rising smoke from the burning antiques. Craven killed the flamethrower as he saw the bundle of money in her hands.

"Is that what I think it is?" he said.

In answer to his question, Cathy reached into the bundle and pulled out a wad of hundred dollar bills. She tossed them into the fire. As Craven made to spring forward, she held the whole bundle towards the flames. "I'll do it!"

Craven froze, fingers twitching on the trigger of the flamethrower. "Don't make me do anything stupid," he said, low and dangerous.

Momentarily forgotten, Gabe reached to the back of his utility belt and removed his final weapon… *the exploderang*. It was a wooden boomerang fitted with a small explosive charge. Suspecting that Craven was about to do something very bad, he flung the boomerang hard, flicking the release on the charge as he did so.

It arced through the air, curving high above the gallery then began to return….

Sensing a movement, Craven turned, bringing the flamethrower upwards….

Too late! The exploderang smacked into the chain holding the chandelier and blew up.

Craven gaped in sudden terror as the weight of metal and crystal fell towards him. There was a mighty crash and he went down.

Gabe didn't waste a second. He pounced on the trapped body of Craven, semi-conscious under the fallen chandelier. Ripping the flamethrower tank off his back, Gabe pieced two holes in it with a tool from his belt. There was the hiss of escaping gas.

With a cry of effort, Gabe heaved the tank towards the window shutter. It ruptured on impact and exploded with enough force to blow a large hole clean through the shutter. It also blasted Gabe back several metres. As he hit the ground, his helmet flew off....

Dazed, he rose to his feet amidst a pall of smoke from the growing fires.

"Angel!" cried Cathy's voice over to his left. "Where are you?"

"Get out!" Gabe cried through the smoke. "Through the shutter!"

"What about you?" she called back.

"I'll be right behind you!"

Gabe saw her turn and dive through the opening. Then he ran back to Craven. With the last of his strength he grabbed the twisted frame and lifted it. The semi-conscious Craven groaned and had the sense to roll to one side. With a cry of effort, Gabe let the chandelier fall back again.

He turned his attention to Craven, who was lying on his back on the floor... staring straight at his unmasked face. Craven's expression was one of shock and surprise.

"You're... you're just a kid."

With that, Craven's eyes rolled into his head as he lost consciousness. Gabe snatched up his helmet from the floor. It was singed on the outside, but otherwise undamaged. He put it on, grabbed Craven under the arms and started dragging him out of the house through the shattered window.

"You're alive!" cried Cathy, running up and helping to haul Craven away from the burning building.

Red and blue flashing lights appeared along the mansion's driveway and Gabe tensed, but Cathy placed a hand on his arm.

"It's okay!" she said. "It's Dad and his men!"

Gabe saw a line of unmarked police cars approaching the house at speed. He was already backing away into the shadows.

Cathy looked at him in surprise. "Wait! My dad will want to talk to you. You're a hero!"

Gabe grinned behind his mask and said, "Cops and guys like me don't tend to get on so well… not in the movies, anyway."

"But…."

Gabe had already melted into the shadows. Cathy turned as the first of the squad cars screeched to a halt. A middle-aged man wearing a bullet-proof vest jumped from the passenger side and threw his arms around his daughter.

* * *

At the boundary wall, Gabe crouched in the shadows and angled a directional mic towards the scene in front of the mansion. Craven was being strapped to a gurney and placed in an ambulance. A police van had just pulled up and an officer emerged.

"We picked them up in the quarry area, Captain Chen," said the officer, his words coming through the speakers in Gabe's helmet. "Five of Craven's men. Pretty beaten up too. Babbling about some kind of masked superhero or something?"

Gabe saw the henchmen cuffed and looking very sorry for themselves in the back of the van.

"What about Big George?" Cathy was asking her dad.

The Captain shook his head. "If he's trying to get out of the country, he hasn't got a chance. All the airports are on the lookout. We'll get him."

Gabe suspected that a man of Big George's means would have his own private jet hidden somewhere. He very much doubted they'd be seeing him or Iain again.

The officers were starting to fan out around the grounds, searching for any more of Craven's men. *Time to leave*, thought Gabe.

He moved cautiously along the security wall, keeping to the darkness. Answering questions about the Guardian Angel wasn't something he wanted to do.

Finally he came to a low point on the wall and pulled himself up.

"Angel!" cried a man's voice. Gabe crouched on the top of the wall, looking round.

Captain Chen was standing just a few metres away, Cathy at his side. "We need to talk!" he said.

Gabe was ready to leap into the darkness…. But a sudden realization came to him. *How had the police known they were at the mansion?* Cathy hadn't been able to get through on her phone. He looked round and said, "You're *whistleblower365*. The person who's been sending me anonymous tips."

Cathy's jaw dropped open as her father nodded. "I've been investigating Big George and his crime links for years," he said. "But he was untouchable. Too …er … well-connected in the police force."

"So you used me," said Gabe.

The Captain shrugged. "I needed someone on the outside. Someone who could stir things up and force Craven out into the open. When I heard about the 'Guardian Angel', I knew I'd found my man."

"So what now?" asked Gabe.

"How about you take off that mask and I thank you face-to-face for what you did tonight?"

Gabe chuckled. "Reveal my secret identity?"

"Like Iron Man!" exclaimed Cathy, clearly eager to see behind the mask.

"Not exactly – Tony Stark is a billionaire," Gabe said patiently. "Some of us so-called 'superheroes' need to protect our families." He turned to leave, but Chen took another step forward….

"Wait!" he called. "Craven's just one of Big George's criminal contacts. We might need some help with the rest!"

"I'll be around," Gabe said, turning his attention to Cathy. "Thanks for your help tonight. I'll look forward to reading your story. Make it a good one."

Cathy grinned back at him. "You bet!"

And then the Guardian Angel was gone, catapulting into the darkness.

Headed for home.

THE END

FICTION EXPRESS

THE READERS TAKE CONTROL!

Have you ever wanted to change the course of a plot, change a character's destiny, tell an author what to write next?

Well, now you can!

'Being Super' was originally written for the award-winning interactive e-book website Fiction Express.

Fiction Express e-books are published in gripping weekly episodes. At the end of each episode, readers are given voting options to decide where the plot goes next. They vote online and the winning vote is then conveyed to the author who writes the next episode, in real time, according to the readers' most popular choice.

www.fictionexpress.co.uk

WINNER
Education Resources
Award for Innovation

TALK TO THE AUTHORS

The Fiction Express website features a blog where readers can interact with the authors while they are writing. An exciting and unique opportunity!

FANTASTIC TEACHER RESOURCES

Each weekly Fiction Express episode comes with a PDF of teacher resources packed with ideas to extend the text.

"The teaching resources are fab and easily fill a whole week of literacy lessons!"
Rachel Humphries, teacher at Westacre Middle School

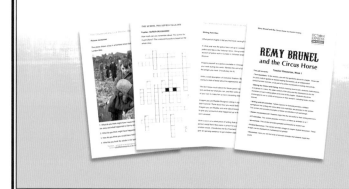

FICTI⬤N EXPRESS

Clock
by Andrew G Taylor

Harry Boyd can stop time – literally. This enables him to live a life of petty crime under the very noses of other shoppers at the Gatesworth Shopping Centre. Then one day, he is surprisingly caught in the act, and everything starts to unravel....

Will Harry and his fellow clock-stoppers succeed in preventing the disaster threatening planet Earth?

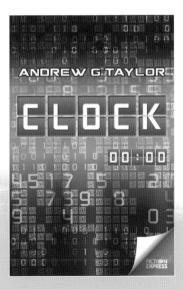

ANDREW G TAYLOR

CLOCK
00:00

ISBN 978-1-78322-555-2

About the Author

Andrew G Taylor was born in New Zealand, grew up in England and now lives in Australia. He's the writer of the 'Superhumans' series and The Adjusters. His work has been shortlisted for the Waterstones Children's Book Award and the Northern Ireland Book Award.

A former teacher who has lived around the world, Andrew uses the places he has visited and the many computer games he's played as inspiration for his writing.